EMERGING 2 READER

P9-DGE-566

The Thirsty Moose

Based on a Native American Folktale

ISBN 0-7696-4050-8

9 780769 640501

50395

EAN

The Thirsty Moose is based on a traditional
Native American story.

Library of Congress Cataloging-in-Publication Data

Orme, David.
    The thirsty moose: based on a Native American folktale/ by David Orme;
    illustrated by Mike Gordon.
            p.cm.—(Lightning readers. Emerging reader 2)
ISBN 0-7696-4050-8 (pbk.)
1. Indians of North America—Folklore. 2. Moose—Folklore. I. Gordon, Mike,
    ill. II.Title. III.Series.

E98.F6075 2005
398.2'089'97—dc22

                                          2004060620

Text Copyright © Evans Brothers Ltd. 2004. Illustration Copyright © Mike
Gordon 2004. First published by Evans Brothers Limited, 2A Portman Mansions,
Chiltern Street, London W1U 6NR , United Kingdom. This edition published
under license from Zero to Ten Limited. All rights reserved. Printed in China.
This edition published in 2005 by Gingham Dog Press, an imprint of School
Specialty Publishing, a member of the School Specialty Family.

Send all inquires to:
8720 Orion Place
Columbus, OH 43240-2111

ISBN 0-7696-4050-8

7 8 9 10 EVN 10 09 08 07 06

The Thirsty Moose

Based on a Native American Folktale

By David Orme

Illustrated by Mike Gordon

GINGHAM DOG PRESS

Columbus, Ohio

It was a very hot day.
Big Moose was thirsty.

He went down to the river.
He drank and drank and drank.

The river water went down and down
and down.

"Stop it!" yelled the beaver.
"I live in this river.
You will destroy my home."

But Big Moose would not listen.
He was still thirsty.

"Stop it!" yelled the muskrat.
"I live in this river.
I will have nowhere to swim."

But Big Moose would not listen.
He was still thirsty.

"Stop it!" yelled the fish.
"We cannot live without this water!"

But Big Moose would not listen.
He was still thirsty.

Along came a little fly.
"You are hurting my friends," he yelled.
"Stop it or I will make you stop!"

Big Moose listened.
He started to laugh.

"Go ahead and try," said Big Moose.

Then, he started to drink again.

The fly flew into
Big Moose's ear.

"I will teach him a lesson," the fly said.
He buzzed and buzzed and buzzed in
Big Moose's ear.

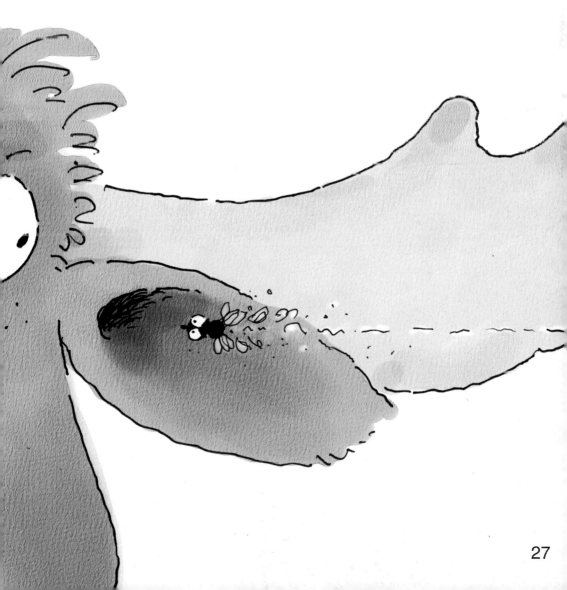

"Stop it!" cried Big Moose.

But the fly would not listen.
Finally, Big Moose could not
take it anymore.
He ran away.

And he never came back
to the river again!

Words I Know

big	live
down	stop
drink	went
hurt	will

Think About It!

1. What was Big Moose's problem?
2. Why were the river animals angry with Big Moose?
3. Why wouldn't the fly listen to Big Moose?
4. Big Moose learned an important lesson at the end of the story. What do you think Big Moose learned?
5. Do you think Big Moose will listen to others in the future? Why or why not?

The Story and You

1. Do you always listen to others? Do you like it when other people do not listen to you?
2. If you were Big Moose, would you have stopped drinking the river water? Why or why not?